For (Hugless) Doug, Liella, Christina and Alessia,
with hugs for Monika and Luka.

www.huglessdouglas.co.uk

HODDER CHILDREN'S BOOKS

First published in Great Britain in 2014
by Hodder and Stoughton

This paperback edition published in 2017

Text and illustrations copyright © David Melling, 2014

The moral rights of the author have been asserted.

All rights reserved

A CIP catalogue record for this book
is available from the British Library.

ISBN: 978 1 444 94903 2

10 9 8 7 6 5 4 3 2 1

Printed and bound in China

MIX
Paper from
responsible sources
FSC
www.fsc.org
FSC® C104740

Hodder Children's Books
An imprint of Hachette Children's Group
Part of Hodder and Stoughton
Carmelite House
50 Victoria Embankment
London EC4Y 0DZ
An Hachette UK Company

www.hachette.co.uk
www.hachettechildrens.co.uk

www.davidmelling.co.uk

HAPPY BIRTHDAY, HUGLESS DOUGLAS

David Melling

Hodder
Children's
Books

One very special day, Douglas was waiting for his friends.

And while he waited he blew up **LOTS** of balloons. 'I hope everyone comes soon,' he said.

'HAPPY BIRTHDAY, DOUGLAS!'

cried his friends as they
burst through the door.

Douglas had so many
presents, he lined
them up in a row.
He was just about to start
opening them when...

'SURPRISE!'

It was Douglas's twin cousins,
Felix and Mash, and the

BiGGEST

PRESENT

he had ever seen!

'Oooh!' said
Douglas.

'Wow, look at all these **PRESENTS!**' said the twins. 'Let's open them!' Felix and Mash bustled past Douglas and helped themselves. 'Oh,' said Douglas. He liked opening presents.

The room was soon a **BiRThDAY MeSS!**
'Don't forget the big one from us,'
giggled the twins.
'It's a doctor's trolley.'

Before Douglas could say thank you,
they tore open the wrapping.

'Oh,' said Douglas again. He was really looking
forward to doing that himself. 'I want to play
outside,' he said, a little sadly.

BOING...

BOING...

BOING...

Douglas felt a little left
out while everyone watched
Felix and Mash push
and pull the trolley about.

'IT'S **MY** BIRTHDAY!'
he said and grabbed his
new pogo stick.
'Watch me bounce.'

WOBBLE...

OOPS...

'**OWWW!**' cried Douglas.
'My leg hurts. And my new pogo stick is broken.
This is my worst birthday ever!'

Poor Douglas sat up
and blew his nose.
'I feel a bit dizzy,' he sniffed.

The twins clambered onto the doctor's trolley.

'NEE-NAW... NEE-NAW.

Felix and Mash to the rescue!'

'It's not that bad,' said Douglas quietly.

'Nonsense!' said Rabbit.

'We'll look after you.'

Douglas tried to stand, with a little help.

But it was no good.

'Hmm,' said Rabbit, 'I have an idea.'

'Now then,' said Doctor Rabbit,
'shhh everyone. I need to listen for
important noises with this listening straw.'

'Hmm. Yes… oh, yes, just as
I thought,' frowned Doctor Rabbit.
'Douglas, you've hurt your leg.
And it's definitely this one,'
she said, pointing.

Felix and Mash unravelled the **BiRThDaY BaNDaGeS** and passed them around.
'We should practise bandage-wrapping before we help Douglas,' said Doctor Rabbit.

'Yes, please,' Douglas agreed.

'It's a bit like wrapping presents, isn't it?' said Douglas.
'Where's Hedgehog?'

'Here,' came a muffled voice. 'I'm fine, thank you!'

Douglas was a little wobbly, so the twins found two long sticks and helped him stand. 'We're sorry you hurt your leg,' said Felix.

Douglas smiled. 'Come on, let's all go home.'

When they arrived there was one more surprise waiting for Douglas. It was a BIRTHDAY TEA PARTY!

After Cow's cake-and-ballo**OOO**on-sandwiches Douglas felt much better. 'Time to play Doctors again!' he said.

Luckily, there were enough
bandages for everyone. Douglas laughed,

'THIS IS MY BEST
BIRTHDAY EVER!'

Surprise present

Balloons

Birthday hug

Birthday bunting

Party hats

Birthday cake

Party twirl

Party tricks

Party poppers

BALLOON PARTY GAME

A birthday party just isn't the same without balloons!
At your next birthday why don't you try this fun game?

1. Mark out **START** and **FINISH** lines

2. Divide your friends into two teams and give everyone a **BALLOON** to hold between their legs

3. Take it in turns to go from the start to the finish line

4. If a balloon touches the floor or **POPS**, that person has to go back to the start line and try again

5. The winning team is the first to complete the course. You could make things trickier by putting obstacles along the way